D0258978

For Jenny, fleetingly known, yet always remembered
and for Zoë Silver, a golden friend – H.R.

For John – A.L.

The sale of this book will help to support the work of SANDS –
Stillborn and Neonatal Death Support.

Text copyright © Hilary Robinson 1999
Illustrations copyright © Anthony Lewis 1999

First published in Great Britain in 1999 by
Macdonald Young Books
an imprint of Hodder Headline Limited
338 Euston Road
London NW1 3BH
10 9 8 7 6 5 4 3

Printed in Hong Kong
British Library Cataloguing in Publication Data available.

ISBN: 0 7500 2688 X

e-mail: Jesus@Bethlehem

Written by Hilary Robinson
Illustrated by Anthony Lewis

MACDONALD YOUNG BOOKS

Let's imagine that Jesus was born today.

The shepherds hear the good news...

on their mobile phones.

Then, hot off the printing press...

Later, on television, everyone sees a news flash.

And via a satellite, in the night sky,
the three kings hear the news.

The shepherds flock to the scene.

The kings travel by private jet.

They bring gifts of gold,

frankincense

and myrrh.

And are stopped at Customs.

Then news spreads on the World Wide Web that a great teacher has been born on Earth.

And e-mails are sent from nation to nation.

And every country sings out to the sound of

the Band of Angels with their new big hit...

And Jesus becomes a new star
in many people's lives.

Yet, it's about two thousand years since Jesus was born. There have been lots of changes. But everything Jesus taught and gave us then, still lives on today.